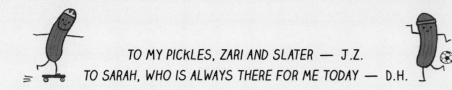

*TO MY PICKLES, ZARI AND SLATER — J.Z.*
*TO SARAH, WHO IS ALWAYS THERE FOR ME TODAY — D.H.*

Owlkids Books acknowledges the financial support of the Canada Council for the Arts, the Ontario Arts Council, the Government of Canada through the Canada Book Fund (CBF) and the Government of Ontario through the Ontario Media Development Corporation's Book Initiative for our publishing activities.

Published in Canada by
Owlkids Books Inc.
10 Lower Spadina Avenue
Toronto, ON M5V 2Z2

Published in the United States by
Owlkids Books Inc.
1700 Fourth Street
Berkeley, CA 94710

Library and Archives Canada Cataloguing in Publication

Zwillich, Julie, author

Not 'til tomorrow, Phoebe / written by Julie Zwillich ; illustrated by Denise Holmes.

ISBN 978-1-77147-172-5 (hardcover)

I. Holmes, Denise, illustrator  II. Title.  III. Title: Not until tomorrow, Phoebe.

PZ7.1.Z85Not 2018          j813'.6          C2017-903872-9

Library of Congress Control Number: 2017943556

The artwork in this book was rendered in ink and colored in Adobe Illustrator.
Edited by: Debbie Rogosin
Designed by: Claudia Dávila

ONTARIO ARTS COUNCIL
CONSEIL DES ARTS DE L'ONTARIO
an Ontario government agency
un organisme du gouvernement de l'Ontario

Canada Council    Conseil des Arts
for the Arts       du Canada

Canadä

Manufactured in Dongguan, China, in October 2017, by Toppan Leefung Packaging & Printing (Dongguan) Co, Ltd
Job #BAYDC45

A    B    C    D    E    F

OWL kids    Publisher of Chirp, chickaDEE and OWL    |    Owlkids Books is a division of    Bayard
www.owlkidsbooks.com                                                                                                        CANADA

# NOT 'TIL TOMORROW, PHOEBE

written by

## Julie Zwillich

illustrated by

## Denise Holmes

Owlkids Books

Phoebe stood beside Mama's bed. She knew she shouldn't wake her up, but she was hungry for pancakes.

"Mama," Phoebe said softly.

Mama's eyes popped open. "Phoebe. What is it?"

"You're honking. And you said we could have pancakes."

Mama rubbed her eyes. "It's called snoring, Phoebe.
And I said we could make pancakes on Friday morning.
That's not 'til tomorrow."

Phoebe frowned. Grown-ups always said *tomorrow* when they didn't want to do something now.

Phoebe would have to make her own breakfast.
Cereal certainly wasn't pancakes, but she knew how
to fix that. She poured a large puddle of maple
syrup right on top. She liked maple syrup. A lot.

Mama came in and did Phoebe's hair. "You could use a haircut, pickle. I'll call and make an appointment."

Phoebe remembered the haircut lady. She had a little dog who wore a funny hat.

"Your haircut will be tomorrow afternoon," Mama told Phoebe while she was getting ready for school. "And we'll get some ice cream after, okay?"

"Okay," said Phoebe. She really liked mint chocolate chip. But she didn't like that word: *tomorrow*.

At school, everyone gathered around Ms. April. "Grab an instrument," she sang. "It's music time!"

Hazel chose maracas, Lucy chose the xylophone, and Nicky grabbed the last drum. The only instrument left was the dented, old trumpet. Phoebe held it to her lips and honked a noisy note. Sounds like Mama, she thought.

"Good news," said Ms. Martha. "Tomorrow some musicians are coming to play their instruments for us." Phoebe frowned. There it was again. Tomorrow.

"And afterwards, we'll have a party. With dancing!" The kids went bananas.

But Phoebe did not go bananas. There was nothing fun about waiting. And that's exactly what you had to do to get to...tomorrow.

Why wasn't anything fun allowed to happen today?

Afternoon circle time cheered Phoebe up a bit. The class sang a counting song in Spanish and played Duck, Duck, Goose.

But just when Phoebe got tagged "goose," Ms. April stopped the game. "Time for the goodbye song," she sang. "We'll play again tomorrow."

Phoebe stomped outside.

"It was finally my turn to be the goose and I didn't get to run," said Phoebe.

"That's too bad," said Mama. "Maybe you'll get a chance tomorrow. Now let's get you to Grammy's."

Tomorrow this, tomorrow that...tomorrow was ruining Phoebe's day!

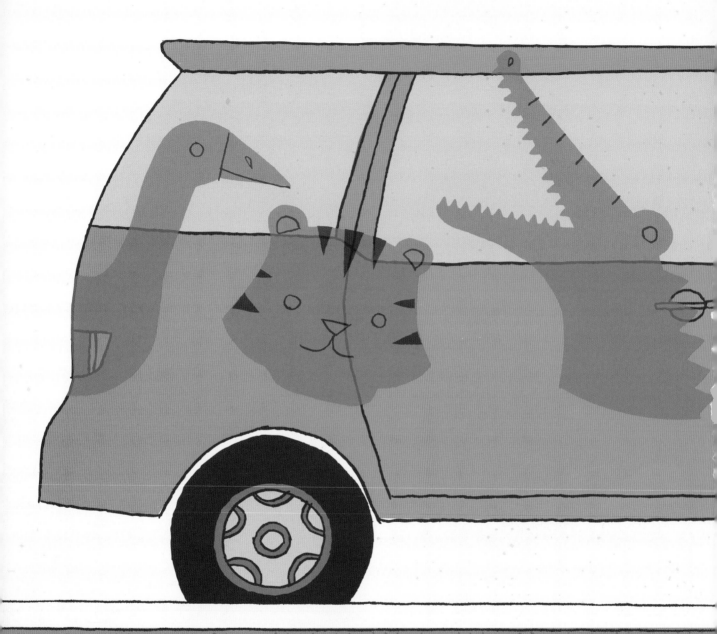

Phoebe looked at her reflection. It stuck out its tongue and crinkled its eyebrows. She wasn't a goose, she was a tiger. Phoebe stepped closer and tried a crocodile face.

Finally, she settled on a big brown bear face with lots of teeth.

GRRR!

Phoebe growled as Mama clicked her seatbelt. She bumped Mama's seat with her back paws.

BUMP
BUMP

"Phoebe, please stop kicking my seat."

"Tomorrow!" Phoebe said in her bear voice.

Mama looked at her in the rearview mirror. She looked mad.

Tomorrow had been causing trouble for Phoebe all day long, and now tomorrow was getting *Phoebe* in trouble. She didn't want to cry, but tears don't always listen, not even to bears.

Grammy came over with cookies. They were stuck
to the upside-down plate. That was a neat trick.

"I wanted to have pancakes and see the haircut lady's dog and eat ice cream and hear the musicians and be the goose, but everyone keeps saying *tomorrow*." Phoebe frowned and wondered if it looked like a smile.

"That's hard," said Grammy, not at all fooled by the upside-down frown.

"I want to take all the tomorrows and throw them away," said Phoebe.

"I don't think you need to do that," said Grammy. "But you *can* add a secret ingredient to make them into todays."

"A secret ingredient?" asked Phoebe. Grammy knew a lot about baking. Not just cookies, but strawberry pies and other things, too.

"Yes. You take a tomorrow and add a good night's sleep to it. When you wake up, it's a today."

Phoebe turned right-side up. "And you could add a pillow and a soft blanket and some good dreams. You could sleep all the tomorrows into todays!"

"Yes," said Grammy. "You could."

"I won't add honks, though," said Phoebe.

Grammy laughed. "You mean like your mama?"

Phoebe nodded.

"No," said Grammy. "You don't need honks."

Grammy walked over to her wall of family pictures. "Phoebe, do you know what happens to all the todays when you're done with them?"

"No," said Phoebe.

"Ah," said Grammy, pointing to a picture of Phoebe when she was a baby. "They become yesterdays."

Phoebe shook her head. She wasn't a baby anymore. "I want to sleep the tomorrows into todays, but you can have the yesterdays."

"I'll add them to my collection," said Grammy.

That night, Phoebe lay in bed with her pillow and her soft blanket. She was ready to try Grammy's recipe.

"Sweet dreams," said Mama.

"That's the most important ingredient," said Phoebe.

Mama looked puzzled. "I don't understand."

"I'll tell you tomorrow," said Phoebe, closing her eyes.